Babushka

Babushka

an old Russian folktale
retold and illustrated by

CHARLES MIKOLAYCAK

Holiday House / New York

Library of Congress Cataloging in Publication Data

Mikolaycak, Charles.
    Babushka: an old Russian folktale.

    Summary: Retells the traditional tale of the old lady
who, having missed her chance to take gifts to the new-
born Christ Child, still wanders leaving gifts for all
children in hopes that, one day, she will come upon Him.
    [1. Folklore—Soviet Union. 2. Christmas—Fiction]
I. Title.
PZ8.1.M598Bab   1984   398.2′2′0947 [E]   84-500
ISBN 0-8234-0520-6

To my Babushkas—Mary, Ann, and Jule.
C.M.

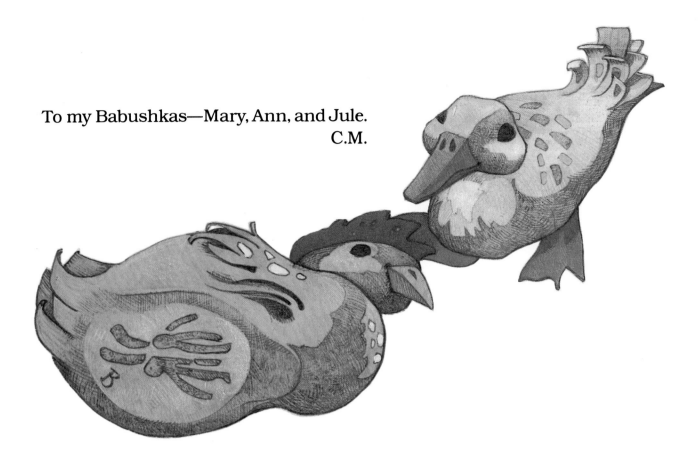

ne night, a long, long, time ago, Babushka was sweeping the floor of her little cottage.

She lived there alone, and all who knew her said she was the best housekeeper in the village.

Every day Babushka swept, polished, and dusted to keep the cottage bright and shining. She worked from the glimmer of dawn to the shadows of night.

And this night was no different. Under the wide Russian sky, Babushka was finishing her chores before she went to bed. The polishing, the dusting, and almost all the cleaning had been done. She opened the door to her cottage to sweep the snow from her doorstep. The cold air reddened her nose and nipped at her ears.

As Babushka swept, the air around her grew warm and fragrant. Raising her head she smelled cinnamon, like the cinnamon in the pies she often baked.

"Is my neighbor Annyushka baking at this hour?" she asked herself. "I doubt it." But the scent became stronger, so Babushka stopped her sweeping and peered down the road.

Through the swirling snow she could
see a procession entering the village. It
seemed longer and more splendid than
any she'd seen for the Tsar. The leader
was riding a humped beast with long
legs. They glided across the snow,
followed by a line of carts and
torchbearers. All moved in silence. Not
the pots hanging from the carts nor
the bells on the animals made a sound.

Babushka stared in wonder at the procession until it stopped at her cottage. At the end were three men who stepped into the snow and came towards her. The first wore a turban. The second had ribbons in his hair. And the third, whose skin was black, wore a many-fringed robe.

The black man gestured toward the sky and asked, "Do you also follow the star?"

Babushka looked through the falling snow and saw a bright, shimmering light.

The man with the turban began, "That star . . ."

". . . will lead us to the King," finished the man with ribbons in his hair.

The black man put his hand on Babushka's sleeve and said, "Come with us. We will take you to the King and you can look into His face and share His delight when He sees the gifts we bring Him."

Babushka was confused. Leave her little cottage? "Oh, no, no, sir," she said. "I have to polish and sweep all day . . ." But before she could finish, the three men turned and stepped into their cart. The black man nodded and as silently as the procession halted, it proceeded on its way. The still-confused Babushka watched until the torches grew dim and disappeared into the darkness.

The next morning, when Babushka awoke, her mind was full of thoughts of dusting, sweeping, and polishing. She jumped from her bed to begin her chores. She went to the corner to get her broom. It wasn't there. Frantically she looked everywhere—in the cupboard, under the bed, even on top of the warm stove.

In desperation Babushka opened the cottage door. There she saw the broom, buried by the night's snow. Wrinkling her nose, Babushka again smelled cinnamon. "Is Annyushka *still* baking?" she asked herself. As she reached for the broom, her sleeve brushed across her nose. The warm, lovely smell of cinnamon was on her sleeve where the black man had placed his hand. Babushka forgot the broom, the sweeping, the dusting, the polishing. She remembered the night before—the torches, the procession, but most of all, the three men.

Babushka's heart beat fast. Abandoning her cottage, she wrapped her scarf around her head and ran down the road, hoping to catch up with the three men who were on their way to see the King.

Many miles from where she started, she met a stranger who told her he'd heard the three men had found the King. He smiled as he said, "And the King was but a child." Upon hearing this, the happy Babushka raced on.

For day after day, year after year, Babushka searched. Every time she gazed into the eyes of a child, Babushka hoped it would be the King.

Her hair lost its golden color and turned silver. Her clothes became worn and tattered and were often repaired. She forgot the cottage that had become covered with snow, the colored walls that had faded, and even the warm stove that had grown cold.

Remembering the three men, she kept sweets or small toys in the pocket of her apron. They would be *her* gifts to the child, the King, when she could look on Him.

At night, a mother, glimpsing into a nursery, might see a strange old figure. But just as quickly, the silent, shadowy shape would be gone. Then the mother would notice a small treat lying on the pillow by her child's head and smell the faint scent of cinnamon that lingered in the air. "Babushka has been here," the mother would sigh knowingly.

Old Babushka's search continued. She visited villages and cities, houses and castles, always leaving behind the scent of cinnamon and a gift. The children would wrinkle up their noses at the warm smell, but they loved the

gifts whether they were a small sweet in shining paper (which they promptly ate) or a wooden chicken or duck made by Babushka herself. They saved the tiny toys for their children, who in turn saved them for *their* children.

So on and on, day after day, today and forever, Babushka continues her search. A baby laughs, the smell of cinnamon fills a room, and a tiny gift appears. We know, and we will always know, Babushka has been there, Babushka who is still seeking the child who was born a King.

This book was set in 13 point Bookman
type by Hallmark Press, Inc. Color
separations were made by Capper, Inc.
It was printed on 80lb. Moistrite Matte
by the John D. Lucas Printing Co.

The illustrations were reproduced in the
same size as originally drawn. They were
created by applying watercolors and colored
pencils to Diazo prints made from the
original pencil drawings.

Thanks to Cathy, Alex, Mark, Glenn, David, and most of all, Margery.